# Treasure Chest Readers

# The Noisy Parrot

**Text by Janine Scott**
**Illustrations by Deborah Rigby**

Published in 2010 by Windmill Books, LLC
303 Park Avenue South, Suite # 1280, New York, NY 10010-3657

Adaptations to North American Edition © 2010 Windmill Books, Copyright © 2008 by Autumn Publishing

Published in 2008 by Autumn Publishing, A division of Bonnier Media Ltd., Chichester, West Sussex, PO20 7EQ, UK

CREDITS: Text by Janine Scott, Illustrations by Deborah Rigby

Library of Congress Cataloging-in-Publication Data

Scott, Janine.
The noisy parrot / text by Janine Scott ; illustrations by Deborah Rigby. -- 1st North American ed.
    p. cm. -- (Treasure chest readers)
Published in Great Britain in 2008 by Autumn Publishing.
Summary: Unable to teach her pet parrot Polly to talk, Penelope Pirate turns to her pirate friends for help.
ISBN 978-1-60754-679-5 (library binding) -- ISBN 978-1-60754-680-1 (pbk.) -- ISBN 978-1-60754-681-8 (6-pack)
[1. Pirates--Fiction. 2. Parrots--Fiction. 3. Humorous stories.] I. Rigby, Deborah, ill. II. Title.
PZ7.S42635Noi 2010
[E]--dc22
                        2009040143

Manufactured in the United States of America

CPSIA Compliance Information: Batch #BW01W: For further information contact Windmill Books, New York, New York at 1-866-478-0556.

an imprint of
**WINDMILL BOOKS**™
New York

Penelope Pirate wanted to teach her pet parrot, Polly, to talk.

"Let's start at the beginning of the alphabet. Repeat after me," said Penelope. "Angela and her awful aardvark, Angus, ate apples from Argentina!"

But Polly Parrot shut her beak and didn't try to speak.

So Penelope Pirate decided to join her pirate friends. They'd know what to do with a parrot that wouldn't talk.

Penelope put Polly in a bright blue boat and paddled to the beautiful Bahamas.

"Blimey, that birdie's got birdbrain-itis!" bellowed a big, bold buccaneer when he saw the bird.

But Polly Parrot shut her beak and didn't try to speak.

The captain's cockatoo, Colin, called
the crew over to check out Polly, who
had crept into a corner to quietly count
creepy-crawly crickets.

"Crikey!" cried the crew. "That crow's
got cuckoo-itis!"

But Polly Parrot shut her beak
and didn't try to speak.

As day dawned, the pirate captain had an idea. "Let's dangle that dim-witted ducky in the dungeon till dinner time. That will make her talk."

"Definitely don't do that!" cried Penelope. "That's dastardly and dangerous!"

So the eager captain had to think of another plan. Before long, he got an encyclopedia and read everything beginning with E to Polly Parrot.

Then, east of the equator, the captain made Polly take an exam. She made eighty-eight errors in eighteen minutes.

"Eeekkk, you've got emptyhead-itis!" exclaimed the captain.

The captain was frightfully furious.
No pirate bird had ever failed before.

"That fowl's got featherbrain-itis!" cried the fiery captain. "There's only one thing for it. Let's go to a far-off frontier and find a fix-it tree."

The captain and Penelope Pirate grabbed Polly. They glided past glaciers in their goatskin kayak.

"Golly," gasped the captain. "I am a galloping goat! I've guessed why Polly's gone gaga. This goose has got goofy goon-itis!"

But Polly Parrot shut her beak and didn't try to speak.

In a haze on the horizon, Penelope Pirate saw Hermit Haven, an island that is very hush-hush. Only pirates have heard of it. So Penelope, the captain, and Polly hopped ashore. Polly ate hundreds of fix-it fruits from the fix-it trees. But that didn't help her at all.

"That hen's got harebrain-itis!" hissed the hysterical captain. "Come on, hawk. TALK!"

But Polly Parrot shut her beak and didn't try to speak.

Then they left the island in an instant.
Penelope and the captain played "I spy"
while Polly idly watched icebergs inch their
way into icy inlets.

But Polly Parrot shut her beak
and didn't try to speak.

After that, Penelope and the captain sang jolly jingles on their journey back to the jetty.

"By jingo! That jay bird's got jittery-itis! It just won't talk," joked the captain.

But Polly Parrot shut her beak and didn't try to speak.

So they anchored the boat, and the captain said kindly, "I'd keep that kooky bird under lock and key!"

Then he waved Penelope goodbye. "Just kidding, kiddo!" he cried. "That bird's kooky but cute!"

Before long, Penelope kayaked past a kingfisher kingdom.

At last, Polly lisped: "I've said very little – a little less than a little – but I really don't have lamebrain-itis. I still like to squawk and I'd just love to talk if it weren't for this laryngitis!"

Then Polly Parrot shut her beak and didn't try to speak.

## LEARN MORE! READ MORE!

Alliteration (when you have a pair, or series, of words or syllables that start with the same sound) can help make a story fun to read, like *The Noisy Parrot*. Here are some more books that use and explore great reading tools like rhyme, rhythm, and alliteration.

**FICTION**
Sierra, Judy. *Wild About Books*. New York: Knopf Books for Young Readers, 2004.

Lobel, Arnold. *The Frogs and Toads All Sang*. New York: Harper Collins, 2009.

**NONFICTION**
Speed Shaskan, Tricia. *If You Were Alliteration*. Mankato, MN: Picture Window Books, 2008.

For more great fiction and nonfiction, go to www.windmillbooks.com.